Copyright © 2016 by LeUyen Pham
Published by Roaring Brook Press
Roaring Brook Press is a division of Holtzbrinck Publishing Holdings
Limited Partnership
175 Fifth Avenue, New York, New York 10010
mackids.com

Library of Congress Cataloging-in-Publication Data

Names: Pham, LeUyen, author illustrator.
Title: The bear who wasn't there / LeUyen Pham.
Other titles: Bear who was not there
Description: First edition. | New York : Roaring Brook Press, 2016. |
    Summary: A picture book inviting readers to join the hilarious search for
    a missing bear.
Identifiers: LCCN 2015034429 | ISBN 9781596439702 (hardback)
Subjects: | CYAC: Bears—Fiction. | Stories without words. | Humorous
    stories—Fiction. | BISAC: JUVENILE FICTION / Animals / General. |
    JUVENILE FICTION / Humorous Stories. | JUVENILE FICTION / Social Issues /
    Friendship.
Classification: LCC PZ7.P4486 Be 2016 | DDC [E]—dc23
LC record available at http://lccn.loc.gov/2015034429

Our books may be purchased in bulk for promotional, educational, or
business use. Please contact your local bookseller or the Macmillan Corporate
and Premium Sales Department at (800) 221-7945 ext. 5442 or by e-mail at
MacmillanSpecialMarkets@macmillan.com.

First edition, 2016
Printed in China by Toppan Leefung Printing Ltd.,
Dongguan City, Guangdong Province

10 9 8 7 6 5 4 3 2 1

The Bear Who Wasn't There

LeUyen Pham

ROARING BROOK PRESS / *New York*

This is the story of the Bear
who wasn't there.

WAIT.

This is not a Bear.

Where is the Bear?

(insert Bear here)

WHAT DID I TELL YOU?
NEVER TRUST A BEAR.
THEY ARE TOTALLY
UNRELIABLE. NOW,
DUCKS, ON THE OTHER
HAND, ALWAYS SHOW UP!
HOW ABOUT I TELL YOU
A NICE DUCK STORY?

Dear Reader,

You will find
the BEAR
on Page 9.

Signed,
ANONYMOUSE

Hmm.
Perhaps we should still
check the next page.

Oops.

The Bear is NOT here.
Let's turn to page 8.

I guess we should go in.

PRIVATE
KEEP OUT
YUP, THE BEAR IS IN HERE. GO ON IN!
SIGNED, ANONYMOUSE
P.S. DON'T WORRY ABOUT THE SIGN ON THE DOOR. JUST COME IN.

Oh dear.
That was definitely
NOT the Bear.

We have to get away from this Duck!
Turn the page.

Have any of you seen a
Bear around here?

A **BOAR?**
I AM A BOAR.

No,
not a BOAR.
A BEAR.

A **PEAR?**
OOH, HERE'S
A PEAR!

No, not a PEAR.
A BEAR.
Is there a
BEAR HERE?

I'M A BARE HARE!
I'M A BARE HARE!

No, not a NAKED RABBIT!
A *BEAR HERE*!

BUT I **AM** A
BARE HARE.

NOT A BARE HARE!

A BEAR *HERE*!!

HERE!!!!!

Oh, forget it.
We're leaving.

Wait! Look!

There is the Bear!
He is hiding behind
the next page!

Turn the page, quick!

This is getting silly.

This book is supposed
to be about a Bear,
and there is no Bear here.

Where is the Author?

WHO, ME?

DO YOU NEED ME?

The book is half over, and we STILL have not seen the Bear.

Let's call everyone in the book together. Maybe the Bear will show up.

I give up.

Where is that Bear?

28

29

WE FOUND HIM!!!
The Bear is here!

Turn around, Bear!

Well, that does it.
We've reached the end
of the book.

I guess there really
IS no Bear here.

Unless . . .

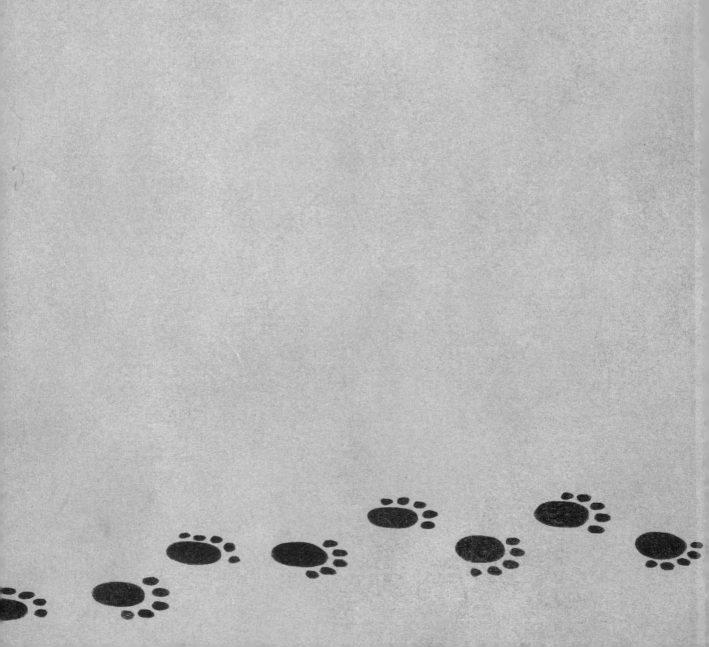